Dear Parent:

Congratulations! Your child is taking the first steps on an exciting journey. The destination? Independent reading!

STEP INTO READING® will help your child get there. The program offers five steps to reading success. Each step includes fun stories and colorful art. There are also Step into Reading Sticker Books, Step into Reading Math Readers, Step into Reading Write-In Readers, Step into Reading Phonics Readers, and Step into Reading Phonics First Steps! Boxed Sets—a complete literacy program with something for every child.

Learning to Read, Step by Step!

Ready to Read Preschool–Kindergarten
• big type and easy words • rhyme and rhythm • picture clues
For children who know the alphabet and are eager to begin reading.

Reading with Help Preschool–Grade 1
• basic vocabulary • short sentences • simple stories
For children who recognize familiar words and sound out new words with help.

Reading on Your Own Grades 1–3
• engaging characters • easy-to-follow plots • popular topics
For children who are ready to read on their own.

Reading Paragraphs Grades 2–3
• challenging vocabulary • short paragraphs • exciting stories
For newly independent readers who read simple sentences with confidence.

Ready for Chapters Grades 2–4
• chapters • longer paragraphs • full-color art
For children who want to take the plunge into chapter books but still like colorful pictures.

STEP INTO READING® is designed to give every child a successful reading experience. The grade levels are only guides. Children can progress through the steps at their own speed, developing confidence in their reading, no matter what their grade.

Remember, a lifetime love of reading starts with a single step!

To Kimberly Coopersburger, as we wait
—H.K.

www.stepintoreading.com

Educators and librarians, for a variety of teaching tools, visit us at
www.randomhouse.com/teachers

Library of Congress Cataloging-in-Publication Data
Kilgras, Heidi.
Cinderella's countdown to the ball / by Heidi Kilgras ; illustrated by Philippe Harchy.
   p.   cm. — (Step into reading. A step 1 book)   SUMMARY: In brief, simple text, Cinderella counts from one magic coach to twelve clock chimes, and back to one glass slipper as she and the prince live happily ever after.
ISBN 0-7364-1225-5 (trade) — ISBN 0-7364-8006-4 (lib. bdg.)
[1. Fairy tales.   2. Folklore.   3. Counting.]
I. Harchy, Philippe, ill.   II. Cinderella. English.   III. Title.   IV. Series: Step into reading. Step 1 book.   PZ8.K5253 Ci 2003 [398.2]—dc21   2002012962

Printed in the United States of America 35 34 33 32 31

STEP INTO READING® STEP 1

WALT DISNEY'S

Cinderella

Cinderella's
Countdown TO THE Ball

by Heidi Kilgras

illustrated by Atelier Philippe Harchy

Random House 🏠 New York

Poor Cinderella.

Poof!
A fairy godmother.

One magic coach.

Two coachmen.

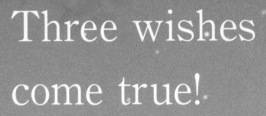

Three wishes
come true!

Four horses.

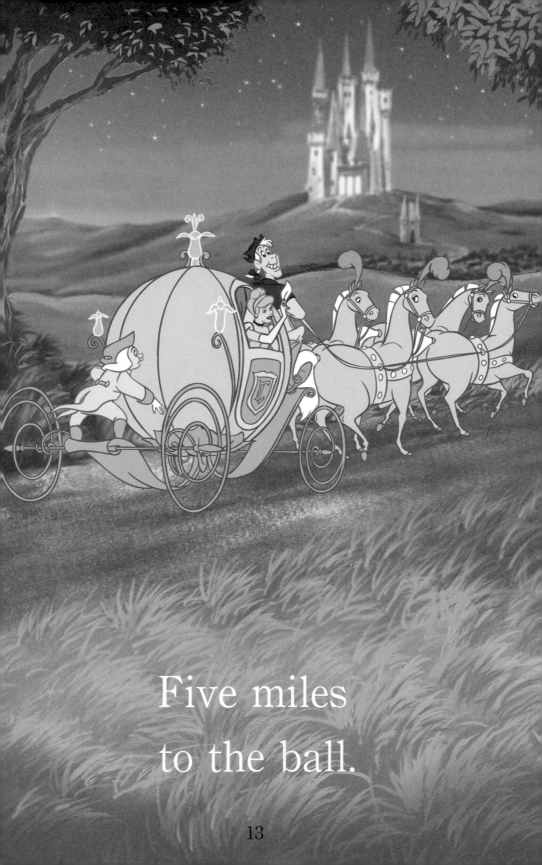

Five miles
to the ball.

Six royal doormen.

Seven men
want to dance.

Eight ladies
wait in line.

The Prince!

They meet.

They dance.
Nine ladies whisper.

Ten fingers touch.

Eleven stars twinkle.

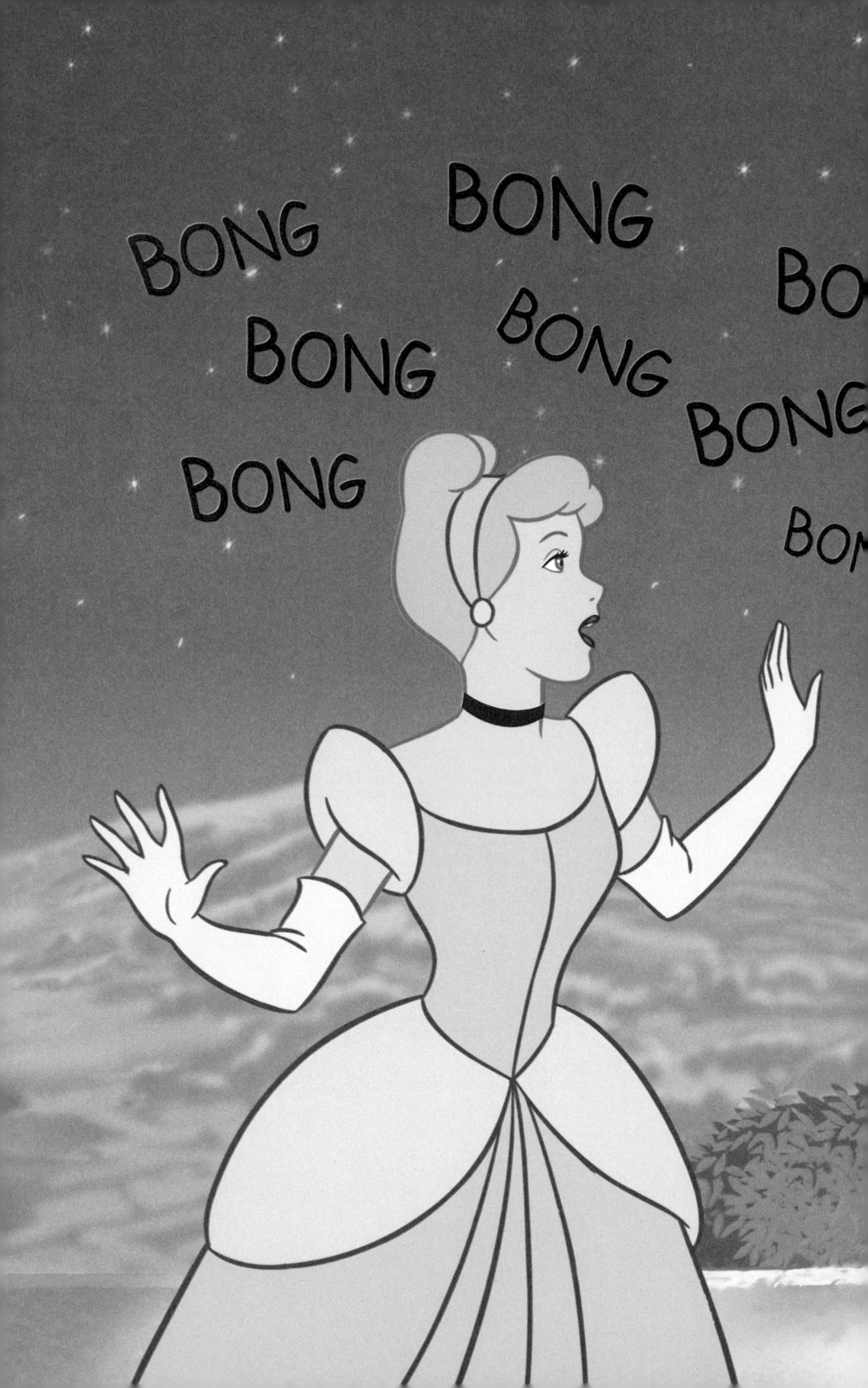
BONG
BONG
BONG
BONG
BONG

Run, Cinderella!

One glass slipper.

Tap, tap.

Too small!

Crash!

The other slipper!

It fits!

Happily ever after!

The End